Echo and the Bat Pack

K!

THE DANCING VAMPIRE

text by Roberto Pavanello
translated by Marco Zeni

Raintree

Raintree is an imprint of Capstone Global Library Limited, a company incorporated in England and Wales having its registered office at 7 Pilgrim Street, London, EC4V 6LB – Registered company number: 6695582

To contact Raintree:
Phone: 0845 6044371
Fax: + 44 (0) 1865 312263
Email: myorders@raintreepublishers.co.uk
Outside the UK please telephone +44 1865 312262.

All names, characters, and related indicia contained in this book, copyright Edizioni Piemme S.p.A., are exclusively licensed to Atlantyca S.p.A. in their original version. Their translated and/or adapted versions are property of Atlantyca S.p.A. All rights reserved.

Text by Roberto Pavanello
Original cover and illustrations by Blasco Pisapia and Pamela Brughera
Graphic Project by Laura Zuccotti and Gioia Giunchi

© 2008 Edizioni Piemme S.p.A., via Tiziano 32 - 20145 Milano- Italy
International Rights © Atlantyca S.p.A., via Leopardi, 8 — 20123 Milano, Italy — foreignrights@atlantyca.it
Original Title: IL MAMMUT FREDDOLOSO
Translation by: Marco Zeni

First published by Stone Arch Books © 2013
First published in the United Kingdom in 2013
The moral rights of the proprietor have been asserted.

Printed and bound in China by CTPS

ISBN 978 1 4062 6203 2 (paperback)
17 16 15 14 13
10 9 8 7 6 5 4 3 2 1

CONTENTS

Hello there!

I'm your friend Echo, here to tell you about one of the Bat Pack's adventures!

Do you know what I do for a living? I'm a writer, and scary stories are my speciality. Creepy stories about witches, ghosts, and graveyards. But I'll tell you a secret – I am a real scaredy-bat!

First of all, let me introduce you to the Bat Pack. These are my friends. . . .

Becca

Age: 10

Loves all animals (especially bats!)

Extremely talented dancer

Michael

Age: 12

Clever, thoughtful, and good at solving problems

Doesn't take no for an answer

Tyler

Age: 11

Computer genius

Funny and adventurous, but scared of his own shadow

Dear fans of scary stories,

Have you ever heard the saying *dance all your problems away*? You haven't? Well, I guess that's not surprising. I only know it because my uncle Skip used to say it! He was a great dancer when he was younger. I never really believed Uncle Skip when he told me to dance all my problems away, but after my latest adventure, I realized that dancing can help you get over a lot of things – sadness, shyness . . . sometimes even the scariest fright of all!

You can't dance? Don't worry, it doesn't really matter! I couldn't dance either, but one day I met someone who told me, "Just go for it!" and I did.

As they say, I have rhythm in my blood! Yuck, blood! That always makes me think of vampire stuff! Why do I always seem to come up with the scariest examples? It must be the mystery writer in me!

I'd better get on with my story. It all started when Becca discovered a sudden passion for dancing. If she hadn't insisted on taking lessons, we would have avoided lots of trouble. On the other hand, the story I am about to tell you could have turned out worse than it actually did. Much, much worse . . .

Chapter 1

Dancing in the rain

It was raining cats and dogs one Friday night in Fogville. It was one of the gloomiest nights I'd seen in a long time – perfect weather for a mystery writer like me!

At the Silvers' house, I glanced out of my attic window and was surprised to see Becca dancing down the empty pavement.

What is Becca doing outside on a night like this? I wondered. She didn't seem to be at all worried about the rain that was soaking her hair and clothes. I watched as she kept dancing in the pouring rain. It was almost as if she thought the lamp-posts on Friday Street were theatre spotlights and the houses were a cheering crowd.

At first, it seemed like I was the only witness to her show. But then I noticed an old woman standing on the dimly lit porch of one of the houses. She was watching Becca dance along. Becca came to a stop in front of the old woman's house. An old basset hound came trotting down the street towards her.

As I watched, the old woman walked down the pavement to where Becca stood. In one hand, she held a short black cane. With her other hand, she held a thin red square out to Becca.

I was instantly reminded of something my mother used to tell me. "Fur-ball," she

would say, "never ever accept fruit flies from strangers!"

I couldn't believe that no one had ever taught Becca such a simple lesson!

By my grandpa's sonar! There was no time to waste! I pushed open the attic window and flew to Becca's rescue. I pulled my wings in close to my sides, just like my cousin Limp Wing, a member of the Aerobatic Display Team, had taught me. Then I nose-dived towards my target before Becca could accept the dangerous gift.

Unfortunately, because it was so dark outside, things didn't go quite as I'd planned. The rain kept pelting my face, making it hard for me tell where I was flying. By the time I reached my target, it was gone! The old lady was back on her porch, and Becca was dancing happily down the street towards our house. I frantically flapped my wings, trying to stop, but it was too late. I couldn't avoid a disastrous crash landing in a big puddle!

As I sat in the cold, slushy water, I could feel my head spinning. Even worse, when I looked up, I saw the dog trotting towards me. Maybe I haven't mentioned this before, but I'm terrified of dogs. I just couldn't move. I was frozen with fear.

"Shoo!" I shouted at it. "Go away, you stupid mutt! Shoo!"

The dog didn't listen. Instead, it started sniffing me from head to toe, tickling me under my armpits.

I looked all around in search of help and met

the eyes of the old woman, who was staring at me and laughing. I glared at her. Luckily, just then, Becca returned. She scooped me up out of the puddle, rescuing me from that terrifying beast.

"Echo!" Becca said. "Have you lost your mind?"

"I'm sorry, Becca," I said, feeling embarrassed. "I thought you were in danger." I looked pointedly at the old woman, who kept staring at us from her porch with an amused look on her face.

"In danger from Miss McKnee?" Becca replied, laughing. "Don't be silly, Echo! She's Fogville's best dance teacher! I was at a friend's house, and I forgot to take my umbrella with me. Miss McKnee saw me jumping around in the rain and decided to lend me one. She even asked me to take lessons at her school! She says I have what it takes to become a dancer!"

Becca proudly held out the red card Miss McKnee had given her. It read:

Alice McKnee's Famous School of Dance – on the dance floor since 1937

I was so embarrassed. I wished the earth would open up and swallow me. Blushing, I turned and smiled at Miss McKnee, who waved in response.

Becca sheltered me under the small borrowed umbrella. "Now let's get home before we both catch a cold!" she said.

Chapter 2

Foul weather

It turned out I was the only one who fell ill. My cold was so bad I couldn't stop sneezing. "Achoooooo!" I sneezed for what felt like the hundredth time.

"Bless you!" Becca said, handing me another tissue.

"Thang you!" I said through my blocked nose. "You are bery gind! A . . . a . . . a . . . Achooooooo!"

"Bless y . . ." Becca started to say.

"Stop!" Tyler interrupted her. "Every time you say 'bless you' he starts sneezing all over again! Just relax, Echo. The cold is just in your head!"

"Jusd in by head?" I mumbled. "Baybe, but by head is throbbing and by dose is running."

"Forget about your nose," Tyler told me. "Concentrate and repeat after me. I feel fine!"

"I veel vi . . ." I tried to say. "Achooooooo!"

"Come on, Echo!" Tyler said. "You're not concentrating hard enough!"

"Give him a break, Tyler!" Michael said. "It's not his fault he's unwell."

"I know that!" Tyler replied. "But I don't want his germs spread all around our room! I don't want to catch it too."

"Why not?" Michael asked. "You'd be able to skip school for a couple of days."

"Yeah, and then Mum won't let me eat anything except crackers and soup," Tyler replied, making a face.

"Go out on the balcony if you're so worried," Becca told him. "It's raining so hard that all the germs will drown."

"Haha, very funny!" Tyler said. He walked over to the window and pressed his face against the glass. A second later, he jumped back with a startled look on his face.

"What happened?" Michael asked. "Did you see the ghost of Echo's cold?"

"Very funny," Tyler muttered. "I thought I saw something across the street."

"That's weird," Becca said. "Who would be out there in this terrible weather?"

"I don't know," Tyler replied. "Look."

Michael and Becca both walked over and joined their brother at the window. Across the street, a moving van was parked in front of an enormous, spooky-looking house.

"That's Shadow Mansion!" Michael said. "I thought it was abandoned."

"Apparently not," Becca said. "Look, they even took down the wood that was boarding up the front door."

"Well, I wish they'd cut the grass," Tyler said. "It looks like a jungle! Who knows what's living in there. I bet there are snakes."

"Maybe even a couple of crocodiles," Becca said, laughing. "Do you want to look, Echo?"

I was curious. There's no denying that. After all, it's not every day new neighbours move in! I got out of bed and flew over to the window to join my friends. Judging by what was being unloaded from the van, our new neighbours were very strange people indeed. As we watched, the movers unloaded an enormous grandfather clock with a skull carved on its face, a couple of rickety trunks, a pile of pots, and an old record player. Nothing else.

The movers quickly carried everything into the run-down, weed-infested house. Then they hurried back outside, climbed into the van, and sped away. The house was once again shrouded in darkness.

Michael, Tyler, Becca, and I all stared at each other in confusion.

"That's weird," Michael said. "I wonder who moved in there."

"Oh, who cares," Tyler said. "I'm sure we'll meet them sooner or later."

"You're probably righ . . . aaachoooooo!" I sneezed.

I didn't know it at the time, but that meeting was going to be much sooner than we expected!

Chapter 3

Hearses in the night

It was a restless night, at least for me. My cold was so bad that I'd decided to sleep in the bed Mr Silver had made for me. (With my nose running so badly, sleeping upside down was totally out of the question!) The thunder and lightning from the storm were so loud up in the attic that I kept falling out of bed!

I'd wanted to sleep downstairs (I'm afraid of thunder, so what?), but Tyler insisted that I snored so loudly it kept him awake. You should hear him snoring! A tractor would be quieter!

Anyway, I was all by myself, hidden under the covers, when my incredibly sensitive ears heard the sputter of an engine, followed by the sound of brakes screeching. I glanced over at the glowing numbers on my alarm clock: 11:33 p.m.

I went to the window to take a peek and almost died of fright! A long black hearse was parked outside Shadow Mansion.

What's going on? I thought. *They just moved in. What is a hearse doing there?*

I kept staring out of the window, waiting for something to happen. Forgetting about my cold, I even opened the window to get a better look. Finally, a tall, thin man dressed all in black got out of the car and looked around calmly. He was holding some kind of lumpy bundle in his arms.

Just then, a cold night breeze tickled my nose. Before I could stop myself, I let out a loud "A . . . choooooo!"

The man turned quickly towards our house. The strange bundle in his arms wriggled in fear. I quickly ducked my head and froze like a statue, not moving a muscle. Finally, I heard the creak of the front door across the street closing.

Phew! I thought, breathing a sigh of relief. Despite my cold, I kept watch for the rest of the night. But nothing else happened. No lights, no noise, nothing. The new neighbours didn't even put their car in the garage.

That's even better, I thought. *When I tell Michael, Tyler, and Becca about someone parking a hearse in front of our house in the dead of night, I'll have proof!*

Unfortunately, I fell asleep at dawn. When Becca came up to the attic to check on me, it was already too late.

"Have you seen Shadow Mansion yet this morning?" I asked as soon as I woke up.

"What about it, Echo?" Becca asked.

"There's a hearse parked in front of it!" I told her.

"Echo, are you feeling okay?" she asked, feeling my forehead. "I think you might be hallucinating."

"I'm not hallucinating!" I protested, flying to the window. "Look!"

But when I got to the window, the words died in my throat. The black hearse I'd seen parked in front of Shadow Mansion was gone, and the windows were boarded up. The house looked completely deserted.

Chapter 4

Street samba

Having your friends think you're a liar is terrible, but having them think you're crazy is even worse.

That whole day I kept watch out of the attic window to see if anything happened in the mysterious house. But it looked emptier than ever.

Midway through the morning my sleepless night caught up with me, and I dozed off. I must have slept like the dead! When I woke up I found myself face to face with a ballerina. It took me a minute to recognize Becca in the dance clothes.

"Becca, what are you are wearing?" I asked.

"My dance uniform! Do you like it?" she asked, posing in her new pink leotard, leg warmers, and ballet slippers. "Miss McKnee wants all her students to dress like this."

"Her students?" I repeated, feeling confused.

"Didn't I tell you? I talked to Mum, and I'm going to start taking lessons with Miss McKnee," Becca explained.

"That's great!" I told her. "You'll make a great ballerina!"

"Oh, no! No ballet for me!" Becca said. "That's too quiet. I'm taking a Latin dance class. Salsa, merengue, bachata, samba! Those are the really fun dances!"

Becca started dancing around the attic to imaginary music. "Come on, Echo! Come here!" she said, holding her arms out to me.

"No way! I'm not dancing!" I replied. I flew up in the air, safely out of reach.

"That's no way for a gentleman to behave!" Becca scolded me. "Will you at least come and pick me up tonight after the first class?"

"Sure," I replied warily. "But no surprises!"

* * *

I convinced Tyler to come with me to meet

Becca after her dance class. He wasn't happy about it, but honestly, I wasn't that excited either. I didn't want to get sucked in to dancing!

When we met Becca, she wouldn't stop talking about Miss McKnee. "She's the world's best dance teacher! Seriously!" Becca said. "She taught us this new dance called the *meneaito*. It's easy. Look."

Even though we were still on the street, Becca started to show us the dance steps. "Stomp your feet in place, clap your hands once to the right, then twice to the left."

By the time we got home, we'd become pretty good at moving together. But our dancing came to a halt when we saw Michael watching us from the upstairs window and laughing.

It's a good thing he's the only one who saw us! I thought.

But I was wrong. Michael wasn't the only one watching us dance. We couldn't see them, but two small, yellow eyes were spying on us from behind a half-closed window in Shadow Mansion.

Chapter 5

Late-night music

Becca wanted the whole family to learn the meneaito after dinner that night. That was my cue to disappear. I wasn't the only one who felt that way. Michael disappeared into his room, Tyler sneaked off to take a nap, and I flew out of the kitchen window for one of my night flights.

My cold was almost gone, and I could smell some delicious scents floating down Friday Street. I could smell the coffee and doughnuts Mrs Silver was making in the kitchen, the scent

of dinner coming from a nearby neighbour's house, and . . . a weird smell coming from Shadow Mansion! I took a deep breath. It smelled like a mixture of beans, pork, coconut, chilli pepper, and pineapple.

I flew out of the window and carefully circled the ancient house. All of the windows were still boarded up, except for the one in the kitchen. I could see a faint yellow light shining through. My heart was racing, but my curiosity won out.

I knew I had to find out who was inside Shadow Mansion.

Flying closer, I hid beneath the kitchen window. Inside, I could hear someone humming in a hoarse voice.

Suddenly, someone flung open the kitchen window and threw out a pan of smelly water. Before I could move, the disgusting water hit me right in the face!

As I sat there in shock, whoever had opened the window slammed it closed again and disappeared.

Soaked to the bone, I flew back home and told the Silver kids what had happened. I must have smelled worse than I realized because they insisted I have a shower right away. After I'd cleaned up, we sat down to figure out what was going on at Shadow Mansion.

"We have to find out who's living in that house!" Michael said.

"Who cares?" Tyler muttered. "Let them cook all the yucky food they want. As long as I don't have to eat it, what does it matter?"

Michael ignored him. "We should take turns watching the house," he said. "Echo, are you feeling well enough to take the first shift?"

I should have known Michael would ask me to work the graveyard shift! I knew what they were all thinking. *Ask Echo. He's up during the night anyway! He's the one with the best hearing!* There was no point in arguing.

* * *

That night, I sat at the attic window watching Shadow Mansion closely for signs of life. It was almost midnight, and I hadn't seen a thing all night.

I was just about to give up when I heard the notes of a sweet, romantic waltz drifting across the night air. Faint light once again spilled through the windows of the old residence.

I glanced at my alarm clock. 11:33 p.m., just like the night before! I opened the window so I could hear better.

Just then, the slow waltz was replaced by a lively Brazilian samba. A couple of windows on Friday Street lit up. The noise must have woken up some of the other neighbours, too. Suddenly, the music stopped, and the lights in the old house went out.

Shadow Mansion looked abandoned once more.

Not our house, though. I could hear thumping noises coming from below. I flew downstairs to see what was going on and found Tyler sleepwalking. Well, sleep*dancing*, actually! He was dancing along to the samba music with his eyes closed. Michael and Becca were watching from their beds and laughing.

We helped Tyler back to his bed, being very careful not to wake him up. (The last time we woke him up from sleepwalking he demanded breakfast in the middle of the night!) After Tyler was back in bed, I told Becca and Michael what I'd seen at Shadow Mansion.

"We have to come up with a plan to get into that house," Michael said.

I was about to agree when Michael's glasses suddenly fogged up. Michael and I stared at each other. We both knew what that meant. Trouble was on its way.

Chapter 6

Dancing apparitions

Trouble came right on schedule.

Over the next week, the weird music and lights continued at Shadow Mansion. On Saturday night, while Tyler was keeping watch, all the lights in the house came on at the same time. Friday Street was once again filled with the notes of a beautiful waltz.

Someone eventually decided to call the police. But when they arrived, they found

Shadow Mansion completely silent and abandoned. Even with people's complaints, the police couldn't do anything more than promise to keep an eye on things.

The next day, the story made the front page of the *Fogville Echo*. The headline read, *Music and Commotion in Abandoned House on Friday Street.*

"We have ghosts as neighbours!" Mr Silver said, sounding amused.

"George, please!" Mrs Silver scolded him. "Can't you see you're scaring Echo?"

She was right. Just hearing the word "ghost" had almost made me choke on the biscuit I was eating. Tyler saved me by hitting me hard on the back (almost breaking it) and making me cough out the piece of biscuit.

* * *

The following week was unusually quiet. I even found time to write. Michael had asked me to write a horror story for him, since he was tired of reading Edgar Allan Poultry's stories for the tenth time in a row.

In the meantime, Becca kept attending her dance classes at Miss McKnee's studio. She was constantly dancing around the house rehearsing her steps and making us practise with her. I found myself rehearsing the merengue, the bachata, the mambo, and even the samba!

I was actually pretty good. *Could I have inherited some of Uncle Skip's talent?* I wondered. *After all, he was the most accomplished dancer of the family!*

But things on Friday Street didn't stay quiet for long. The strange music and lights returned the following Monday.

The *Fogville Echo* quickly picked up the story. According to the front-page article, all of the witnesses were women, and each one told the same story. She was woken in the middle of the night by a piece of heartbreaking music. The next thing she knew, she was standing in front of a stranger who made her waltz with him. In the middle of the waltz, a strange, brightly coloured animal barged into the room, the music stopped abruptly, and the mysterious gentleman vanished into the night. Then the music changed to a lively samba. None of the women could remember anything after that.

As if that wasn't bad enough, Becca managed to make things even worse. Coming back from dance class that afternoon, she spun into the living room. "One-two-three, one-two-three," she chanted. "Miss McKnee taught us the waltz tonight!"

"The waltz?" I repeated. "But I thought you were taking a Latin dance class."

"I was, but the waltz is Miss McKnee's speciality," she explained as she danced around the room. "She was a champion back in the day!"

"Boring!" Tyler grumbled. "Is your dance obsession ever going to end?"

"End?" Becca repeated. "This is just the beginning!" She reached into her bag and pulled out an old record called *Dancing to the Vienna Waltz*. "Miss McKnee lent this to me so I can practise. I'm going to start right now!"

Becca dug out Mr Silver's old record player and put on the record. The sounds of the waltz immediately filled the house. Tyler, Michael, and I tried to quietly sneak out. Mr and Mrs Silver, on the other hand, started dancing around the living room furniture.

Maybe Becca was right. That was just the beginning.

It's raining mints

Becca didn't give up. She spent the whole night trying to teach us to dance. First, she tried (unsuccessfully, I should add) to show Tyler how to waltz.

Finally she gave up. "A mummy could dance better than you!" she told her brother, looking exhausted.

Tyler curled up on the sofa and squeezed a pair of cushions against his ears, trying to ignore her.

Then it was Michael's turn. He was better than Tyler, but clearly not interested. He kept reading his latest Edgar Allan Poultry novel, even as he was dancing.

Finally it was my turn. I was nervous, but according to Becca, I was the best dancer of all!

"It's too bad that you're so tiny, Echo," she told me. "Otherwise you'd make a perfect partner!"

After Becca finished with our dance lessons, she disappeared upstairs to practise in her room. Mr and Mrs Silver had gone out to dinner, and the boys and I stayed downstairs. None of us wanted to be captured by Becca again.

Even from upstairs we could hear the waltz music and Becca chanting, "One-two-three, one-two-three." I decided to get some fresh night air. Sometimes having a pair of wings is so nice!

I'm not sure how long I was gone, but as I glided back towards the Silvers' house, I saw something that made my blood curdle. A tall, lanky man dressed in black was slowly creeping up the driveway and heading for the back door!

Scaredy-bat! I recognized him right away. It

was the same man I'd seen climbing out of the hearse in front of Shadow Mansion! Suddenly, the man stopped and looked up at Becca's brightly lit window, where I could hear music of the waltz still playing.

Suddenly I recognized the song. It was the same music I'd heard coming from Shadow Mansion at night!

While I tried to figure out what to do, the man opened the back door (Mrs Silver is always reminding us to lock it!) and slipped inside like a shadow.

By my grandpa's sonar! I had to warn my friends!

I flew into the

living room as fast as I could. When I got there, I found Tyler and Michael still sitting on the sofa.

"I just saw someone sneak into the house!" I exclaimed. "I think he went up to Becca's room!"

"Are you sure?" Michael asked. He immediately put down the book he'd been reading.

"Positive!" I replied.

"What are we going to do, Michael?" Tyler asked, looking scared.

"We have to rescue our sister!" Michael declared. "Grab one of the cushions from the sofa!"

"Are you crazy?" Tyler yelled. "You want to take on some intruder with a couple of cushions?" I'd never seen him look so horrified.

"All we have to do is scare him off, not hurt him!" Michael insisted. "Echo, see what else you can bring."

I looked around and saw a bowl of mints

sitting on the table. I immediately thought of a trick my cousin Limp Wing had taught me – the winged machine gun.

I remembered what he'd told me. *Every time you flap your wings, fire some ammo at your target. If you get really good at it, you can fire as many as 60 shots per minute!*

There was no time to waste! Even though I was scared, I filled my wings with mints and revved up for the battle to save Becca.

Upstairs, we heard the bedroom door open and close very quickly.

"Let's go!" Michael declared, starting up the stairs.

We hurried up the stairs and stopped outside of Becca's bedroom door. Inside, we could hear her talking to someone. She laughed, and the music grew louder.

"Echo," Michael told me, "go outside and circle the house. As soon as the lights go out, you fly in through the window. We'll go in through the door and capture him in the middle!"

I obeyed Michael's command and flew outside. As I hovered outside Becca's window, I could see the shadows of Becca and the stranger dancing together. Suddenly, the lights went out. That was the signal!

I flew into the room shooting mints left, right, and centre. On the other side of the room, Tyler and Michael furiously swung their cushions. Someone hit the record player, and the music screeched to a halt.

I heard a familiar voice yell, *"Pan de Sucre!* Quick, Master! Let's go!"

The man elbowed his way to the door and

rushed down the stairs with his mysterious helper. Before we could follow, he disappeared.

When Michael turned on the lights, I looked at the time. 11:33 p.m.

Chapter 8

Surprise coffin

You would have thought Becca would be grateful to us for saving her. Think again! Not only did she not thank us, she called us all sorts of names for scaring away the only decent dance partner she'd been able to find.

"Who's going to be my partner at the recital now?" Becca demanded. "You guys ruin everything!" She wouldn't even talk to us anymore after that.

"I can't believe her!" Tyler grumbled. "We risk our lives to save her and all she does is shout at us!"

"Did anybody get a good look at the man at least?" I asked.

"Nope," Tyler said. "It was too dark. I did hit his bird with my cushion, though."

"Bird?" Michael repeated. "What bird?"

"I found this on the bedroom floor," Tyler said, holding up a yellow feather. "I figured that's what that strange animal with him was."

"Well, at least we learned something," Michael said. "We know one of them is a bird. All we have to do now is find out who the other one is. And there's only one way to do that."

Tyler and I exchanged a worried glance.

"You want to take a tour of Shadow Mansion tonight, don't you?" I asked.

"Bingo!" Michael replied.

* * *

As soon as Becca went to bed, Michael, Tyler, and I sneaked out of our house and over to Shadow Mansion.

"It looks like the door is open," Michael whispered, as we walked up the front steps. He leaned on the handle, and the door swung open, creaking eerily. The noise echoed throughout the empty hallway.

Michael, Tyler, and I stuck close together as we crept slowly inside. Tyler turned on the torch he'd brought with him and shone it around the room. We could see antique furniture, curtains, and glass chandeliers standing motionless under a thick layer of cobwebs and dust. In the living room a grandfather clock with a skull carved into its centre stood guard silently.

"Hey, can you smell that?" Tyler whispered.

I took a deep sniff. It was the same mix of meat, chilli pepper, and tropical fruit that I'd smelled a few nights before. But before I could tell Michael and Tyler, we noticed a faint light shining at the top of a flight of stairs.

"Go and have a look, Echo," Michael ordered.

Even though I was terrified, I knew I had to be brave. I fluttered up the staircase and peeked around the corner.

I immediately wished I hadn't. In the centre of the room, a polished, black coffin rested on a pedestal surrounded by candles. Scaredy-bat!

I don't know where I found the courage to do so, but I flew closer and looked at the plaque on the cover. It read:

COUNT ALARIC CARPATIAE

Next to the coffin, a fat, multicoloured parrot was snoring peacefully on an iron perch. She was wearing a brightly coloured skirt and some kind of headdress full of fake fruit.

So that's the animal our mystery man is always carrying around! I thought.

Just then, the grandfather clock chimed twice. I quickly flew out of sight. And it's a good thing I did!

As I watched, the bird woke up, shook her feathers, and flew over to the coffin. Using her beak, she tapped on the lid three times.

"Wake up, Master!" the parrot said. "It is a beautiful night. Perhaps you will find her this time!"

From my hiding spot, I could see the lid on the coffin slowly begin to rise. A long, pale hand emerged and clasped the side of the coffin.

I had seen enough. I bolted back to my friends.

"Psst, Echo!" Michael whispered. "We're over here!" He and Tyler were anxiously waiting for me at the bottom of the big marble staircase.

"There's someone coming," I whispered frantically. "We have to leave while we still can!"

"That's the best idea I've heard so far!" Tyler said, turning to run.

But none of us had taken Becca into account.

When we turned and saw her sneaking through the front door, we realized that we were in big trouble.

She must have had the same idea we did to poke around our neighbour's house! I realized. I turned to Michael and Tyler. "We have to warn her before it's too late!" I said. I didn't want Becca to run into what I'd seen upstairs.

"She won't listen to you," Michael told me.

"I have to try!" I said, hurrying towards her. "Becca! You have to get out of here! You're in danger!"

Chapter 9

Saved by the bird

Becca ignored me. She waved her hand, as if she was trying to shoo away a fly. It was like she was hypnotized! Then she suddenly smiled. Fearing for the worst, I turned around. Sure enough, Count Alaric was walking slowly down the stairs.

There was no doubt about it now. That fellow was a . . . a . . . I was afraid to even think the word!

I rushed back to the staircase, where Michael and Tyler were still hiding. I was so scared I couldn't even speak! Tyler looked as terrified as I felt. He couldn't stop biting his nails. Michael, on the other hand, was perfectly calm.

"That's the dancer from earlier, isn't it?" he asked.

"I think so," I replied. Tyler let out a frightened whimper.

"Calm down," Michael said. "I think I know what he has in mind. He'll put on a record, probably a waltz. Then he'll ask her to dance."

"That's it?" Tyler said. "And then what?"

"And then we'll see!" Michael snapped. "What do you think I am, a psychic?"

"I swear, if that big bully hurts her . . . I . . . I'll have him for breakfast!" Tyler said.

Michael and Tyler clearly didn't realize what Count Alaric really was.

Maybe I should tell them, I thought. But I decided to keep quiet. Knowing what we were dealing with could scare them to death!

We all needed to be thinking clearly if we were going to save Becca. After all, I was well aware what vamp . . . well, people like him did to their victims. I had to be ready to act. A minute too late, and it would be a disaster!

Everything went just like Michael had predicted. Count Alaric kissed Becca's hand and walked her into an empty ballroom. He clapped his hands twice, and his turban-wearing parrot fluttered into the room and lit several candles. The flickering flames barely lit the big room. Long, dark shadows danced all around.

Count Alaric went to the record player and

placed a record on it. The air was immediately filled with the music of a waltz we were all very familiar with. It was the same music we'd heard floating down Friday Street every night.

The count held out his hand to Becca, and they began to dance. Watching Becca twirl so gracefully was almost enough to make me forget the danger she was in.

Suddenly, I noticed a dark shadow peering through the big living room window. I looked

closer. The shape was familiar. I turned to warn Michael and Tyler, but they were more concerned with Count Alaric, who was now smiling at Becca and baring two sharp fangs!

"L-look at those teeth!" Tyler stuttered. "Wait a minute, those are the teeth of a . . . a . . ."

"Echo! What did you see in that room? Are you sure you told us everything?" Michael demanded.

But it was too late for explanations. The Count was staring at Becca's neck. His mouth was already open. I was about to jump at him when the music suddenly screeched to a stop. We heard a dog barking outside.

"*Pan de sucre!*" the parrot blurted out from her spot on the record player. "Master, can't you see that she's just a little girl? She can't be the one!"

Count Alaric smiled sadly, then put his hand in his pocket and pulled out two raw carrots. He handed one to Becca and bit into the other one himself, looking disappointed. With that, he turned and walked sadly back up the stairs.

The bird shook her head and changed the waltz to some lively Latin music. "Do you know the samba?" she asked me, pulling me into a wild dance. "It's good to get rid of your sadness! Let yourself go! Go for it!"

It was impossible to resist the music! I started dancing, and so did Michael, Tyler, and Becca. We all danced 'til we couldn't dance anymore! One by one, we dropped to the floor in exhaustion.

"I think I owe you all an explanation," the parrot said, shaking her feathers. "Follow me into the other room. I'll make you a snack and explain everything."

That was all it took to get us moving again. At the mention of the word snack, even Tyler, who had fallen asleep as soon as he hit the floor, awoke immediately.

"Did someone say something about a snack?" he asked.

Chapter 10

Flaming rice!

The parrot led us into a kitchen that was also lit by candles. The smell of spices and tropical fruit became even stronger.

"*Pan de sucre!* I almost burned it!" the bird shrieked, quickly turning off the stove. "First of all, let's introduce ourselves. My name is Ipanema, and I come from Brazil. From Rio de Janeiro to be exact!"

The Silver kids and I introduced ourselves

as well and explained that we lived across the road. As we spoke, Ipanema handed us plates filled with some strangely coloured rice.

"This is Carnival Rice. It's one of my specialities," she told us. "It's made with beans, pineapple, peppers, dried plums, Brazilian hazelnuts, coriander seeds, pepper, and hot paprika. Veeery hot! Be careful, it burns like fire!"

"I love hot food!" Tyler said, shoving a spoonful of rice into his mouth. What a mistake! His face immediately turned bright red! Rushing over to the sink, Tyler frantically splashed water into his mouth to soothe the burning.

Ipanema watched him, chuckling in her husky parrot voice. "You must be a brave group to sneak into an empty house in the middle of the night, dance with a stranger, and eat food made by a talking parrot!" she exclaimed.

"We're used to talking animals," Tyler said, motioning to me. His face had almost returned to its normal colour. "Echo can even write."

"He's also an amazing Samba dancer!" Ipanema said. "*Pan de sucre!* Where did you learn how to dance like that?"

"Becca taught me," I replied.

"Really?" Ipanema replied, looking impressed. "Ah, dancing! My life's joy and my master's ruin!"

"By the way," Michael said, pushing his plate aside, "why don't you tell us about your master?"

"Sí, sí, that's why I'm here," the parrot said. "The man Becca was dancing with is named Count Alaric. He is a vampire count from Transylvania. Don't worry, he's totally harmless. He hasn't bitten anyone in more than half a century! He became a vegetarian when she disappeared."

"Who is she?" Becca asked, looking intrigued.

"*Pan de sucre!* The woman who broke his heart, of course!" Ipanema exclaimed. "She was the greatest dancer he'd ever met! They met one evening at a party and danced together all night long! Then, while the orchestra was playing *The Blue Danube*, he smiled at her. The woman, who was probably in love with him already, saw his sharp fangs. She was terrified and ran away, forever leaving him in the middle of the dance."

Ipanema shook her head sadly. "Ever since then, Count Alaric has been looking for that lady. He tries to dance the waltz with every woman he meets, hoping to find his lost partner and take her with him."

"But he hasn't found her yet?" Michael asked.

"He's still searching," Ipanema replied.

"How did you get involved in all of this?" Becca asked.

"Count Alaric saved me from a circus," Ipanema explained. "I was stuck performing

as the talking parrot. Since he rescued me, I promised to help find his missing dance partner. When I do, he'll take me back home to Brazil. Unfortunately, we haven't had any luck so far."

The colourful parrot looked over at Becca. "Then the other night he heard the music that

has been tormenting him for years coming from your window," she said. "He was certain he had finally found his long-lost partner. But tonight he realized he had made another mistake. My poor master!"

"Even if Count Alaric does find that woman,

how does he think he'll be able to recognize her after all this time?" Michael asked.

"That's what I've been telling him for years," Ipanema said. "But he insists he'll be able to. Every time I bring it up, he says, 'All I need is one dance with her. Even if that isn't enough, her hair will tell the truth.'"

"Her hair?" Michael asked. "What does that mean?"

Unfortunately, that was all Ipanema would tell us about her master. After we finished eating, she shooed us out of Shadow Mansion. As we walked back to the Silvers' house, Michael's glasses fogged up. I knew what that meant. Our mystery was far from over.

Chapter 11

Watch your toenails

The next day was a Saturday, and the Silver kids didn't have school. But that didn't mean we had the day off. Michael immediately put Tyler in charge of research.

"Tyler, see what you can find out about vampires," Michael said. "I want to find out what kind of mark they leave on the people they meet."

"Isn't Becca's face enough proof?" Tyler replied. "Pale, wrinkled, lots of grey hair."

"You have wrinkles!" Becca snapped back. "And besides, I don't have a single grey hair!"

"Come on, Tyler!" Michael pressed him. "We need to figure this out if we want to solve the mystery of our new neighbour."

"Fine," Tyler said, sighing loudly. He sat down in front of his computer and got down to business. "Let's try 'vampires and side effects.'"

Seconds later, the screen was filled with results. Tyler clicked on one of the links and we all leaned over his shoulder.

Michael read aloud. "'People who claim to have met a vampire and managed to avoid his sharp teeth, still bear obvious marks. Some of these marks disappear after two or three months, while others can be permanent. The most common are: unusually fast growing toenails, persistent itching in the neck, sleepwalking during the full moon, and grey hair.'"

"See, Becca?" Tyler teased her again. "It says right here that vampires give you grey hair."

"Leave me alone, Tyler," Becca said, rolling her eyes. "I'm going out."

"Are you going polka dancing with a werewolf?" Tyler asked, cracking himself up.

"Very funny!" Becca snapped. "For your information, I'm going to Miss McKnee's house. I need to return the record she let me borrow."

Michael looked at her sharply. "Can I see that record before you take it back, please?" he asked.

"Sure," Becca said, handing him the old record sleeve. It was green with golden scrolls on it.

Michael's eyes opened wide with shock. "This is the same record Count Alaric was playing!" he exclaimed.

"That's true!" I said, looking at him with excitement. "I saw it too."

"So what?" Becca replied. "It's probably just a coincidence."

"Maybe," Michael replied thoughtfully. "But there's one more loose end we need to tie up. Tyler, could you look up Alice McKnee on the computer?"

We all moved closer to the screen as Tyler typed frantically. He clicked on an article about Miss McKnee.

Michael read the article aloud. "'Alice McKnee was a former dance champion, three-time winner of the 'Heel-Toe' competition, winner of the Grand Jury Prize as best dancer in the waltz category, and winner of the 'Glass Slipper' award in the same category.'"

"So what? You can find that information on the school brochure!" Becca protested.

"'At her peak, Alice McKnee suddenly

retired and withdrew from all competitions,'" Michael continued. "'McKnee never provided an explanation for her retirement and virtually disappeared for several years.'"

He looked at Becca pointedly. "Does your brochure say that too?"

"Keep reading," Becca replied, finally starting to understand.

"'When she finally resurfaced, McKnee decided to become a full-time teacher. She opened the famous Alice McKnee School of Dance, which she is still running to this day,'" Michael finished.

"You're saying you think Miss McKnee could be . . . no, that's impossible!" Becca said. "It's crazy!"

"It's not that crazy," Michael insisted. "It says right here that she retired suddenly without ever providing an explanation. What other explanation could there be?"

"Why don't you ask her?" Becca suggested.

"Yeah, right," Tyler muttered. "Like she's going to tell us what happened."

"I think I know how we can get her to talk," Michael said. "But only if Echo gives me a hand."

Chapter 12

Michael the detective

Michael and Tyler, who had dressed for the occasion as a private detective, went with Becca to her dance class at Miss McKnee's that evening. I would have gone with them, but I was busy carrying out the assignment Michael had given me. For once, it wasn't a risky one.

"Miss McKnee, my brothers would like to ask you some questions," Becca said, looking embarrassed. "It's, uh, for the school newspaper."

"Please, have a seat," Miss McKnee said, smiling at them. She looked amused by Tyler's mirrored sunglasses and yellow trench coat.

"Wow! You've won so many prizes!" Tyler exclaimed, admiring the cups, medals, and plaques that covered the walls. "Did you win them all by yourself?"

"Not quite," Miss McKnee replied. "You see, young man, in order to dance the waltz, you need a partner!"

Tyler opened his mouth to ask another question, but Becca elbowed him in the stomach.

Michael took advantage of the moment. "Do you recognize this?" he asked, handing Miss McKnee the *Dancing to the Vienna Waltz* record.

"Of course!" the dance teacher replied. "It's the record I gave Becca to practise with."

"What if I told you that our neighbour has the exact same one?" Michael asked. "Would you believe that?"

"Oh, I suppose that's possible," Miss McKnee said. "It was a very popular record back in the day."

"We read in your biography that you retired from dancing very suddenly," Michael said, "Can I ask why?"

"I had an . . . incident," Miss McKnee said, starting to look uncomfortable. "An emotional shock of sorts. It took me years to get over it. Fortunately, I had my school!"

Michael studied her intently. "That lock of white hair," he said. "Does it have anything to do with your incident? Let's say . . . a big scare?"

Miss McKnee stiffened. "What kind of a question is that, young man?" she demanded.

"Is that the kind of news you publish in your school newspaper? I think that's enough questions. If you'll excuse me, I have a lot to do. The school's recital is coming up soon."

But Michael didn't give up. "Please, just one more question," he said. "I saw you poking around Shadow Mansion with your dog last night. What were you doing?"

Miss McKnee's face went pale. "I walk my dog every night. But I definitely don't go poking around empty houses! I'm afraid you're mistaken, young man."

"Do you know a parrot named Ipanema?" Michael asked.

"I've never heard of it," Miss McKnee replied.

"That's odd," Michael said, "since it seems you two have a friend in common. Does the name Count Alaric ring a bell?"

If the chair behind her hadn't broken her fall, Miss McKnee would have fainted. She was white as a sheet. Her dog looked up at her, whimpering.

"Don't be afraid," Becca said. "We want to help you."

Just then, I came flying through the

window, followed closely by Ipanema. We performed a magnificent entrance flight, if I do say so myself! But no one applauded for us. On the contrary,

the dog started barking like mad, and Miss McKnee stared at us in shock.

"Let me introduce you to Ipanema. She's the personal assistant of Count Alaric, who is currently living in Shadow Mansion," Michael said. "And don't tell me you didn't know."

"I suspected it," Miss McKnee finally admitted with a sigh. "That particular waltz in the middle of the night was too strange to be a coincidence."

Ipanema flew over to Miss McKnee. "*Pan de sucre!*" Ipanema exclaimed. "I have heard so much about you!"

"How is the count?" Miss McKnee asked.

"Terrible," Ipanema told her sadly. "He has spent all these years looking for you. But now, maybe his journey will finally be over."

Miss McKnee sighed. "I've got nothing to lose," she said. "Just tell me what I have to do."

"When did you say the Debutante Ball is going to be?" Michael asked.

"On Saturday," Miss McKnee replied. "In exactly three days."

"Perfect!" Michael said. "That gives us 72 hours to go back in time!"

Chapter 13

The flying samba

When Miss McKnee told us where she planned to have the recital, we were speechless. She wanted to hold it in the very place where she and Count Alaric had danced all night long many years before. Well, at least 'til 11:33 p.m., when their last waltz had been interrupted.

You read that right. She wanted to have it at Shadow Mansion!

I figured she had to have a plan, so we rolled up our sleeves and got down to business.

Ipanema and I even managed to plan a little surprise.

Despite all the excitement, I was nervous. *What if something goes wrong?* I thought.

I shouldn't have worried. On the night of the recital, everything was perfect. Tyler was in charge of the music and the lights. Michael was in charge of the snack counter. Miss McKnee was greeting the guests.

Ipanema and I perched on the branch of a large tree to go over the final details of our surprise.

"When are you going to do it?" I asked Ipanema.

"At the time we planned, of course!" she replied.

"Do you have matches?" I asked.

"Of course!" she said. "I already set up the candles."

"But what about the –" I started to ask.

"Relax, Echo!" Ipanema said, realizing how nervous I was. "Everything will be fine. What about you? Are you sure you'll remember the steps?"

"That's easy," I replied. "One-two-three, one-two-three . . ."

From my spot in the tree, I watched Miss McKnee's students perform their dances. When Becca's group was on, I clapped so hard that my wings were sore!

Then it was our turn. Tyler put the music on, and we started our midair performance – the Flying Samba!

At first, the guests stared at us in shock. But little by little, they started to enjoy our performance. By the end, they were clapping and cheering. It was a real success!

The *Fogville Echo* even printed an article about us the next day! The headline read, "Even Animals Learn to Dance with Miss McKnee!"

When the buffet started, everyone forgot about us and tucked in to the soft drinks and snacks. I glanced at my watch. It was almost time. Ipanema winked at me and flew to the house.

As soon as the guests finished eating, McKnee invited everybody, adults and children, to join her on the dance floor for a spectacular final waltz.

Chapter 14

The last dance

As soon as the notes of the waltz began to play, dancers swarmed the dance floor. Even Mr and Mrs Silver were there, dancing and staring into each other's eyes like a couple of college sweethearts.

As everyone danced, I watched the sky with concern. It looked like rain, but people didn't seem to care. They just kept dancing happily. Suddenly, a bolt of lightning cracked the sky, briefly illuminating a tall, lanky figure standing on the steps of Shadow Mansion. No one noticed.

At the edge of the dance floor, one lonely dancer stood waiting. The figure on the stairs jolted in surprise when he saw her. He started walking towards her. When he was close enough, he held out a hand to touch her lock of white hair. Then he smiled gently, baring a pair of sharp fangs. Another flash of lightning lit up Count Alaric's face.

"Help! A vampire!" someone screamed.

At that exact moment, the rain came pouring down. All the couples sought shelter under the buffet tent. All except one, that is. Unconcerned with the rain and lightning, the couple kept dancing to the notes of their favourite waltz.

"That's a real vampire!" someone squealed.

"And that's Miss McKnee!" someone else added.

No one moved. All the guests stood, mesmerized, as Count Alaric and Miss McKnee danced. Ipanema, the Silver kids, and I all held our breath.

I looked at my watch. It was 11:32 p.m.! One more minute, and the curse of the interrupted dance would be broken forever!

Just then, a violent flash of lightning

struck Shadow Mansion. The power went out, bringing the music to an abrupt stop. The two dancers stopped and stared at each other as the rain kept falling. By my grandpa's sonar! This was a disaster!

"Do something, Echo!" Ipanema demanded. She quickly went to work lighting the candles she'd placed around the garden. "If the music doesn't start again, it's all over!"

Count Alaric looked terrified at the idea of seeing his tragedy unfold once again. Miss McKnee stared back at him as the seconds ticked away. Ten, nine, eight . . .

A light bulb went off in my head. I knew exactly what to do, but I didn't have much time! Thankfully, my cousin Limp Wing had taught me hundreds of aerobatic tricks. I knew just which one to use – the Spinning Top!

I grabbed the needle of the record player with my feet and started spinning. Time was almost up. Three . . . two . . . one . . . At 11:33 p.m. sharp, the notes of the familiar waltz filled the air around us once more!

Count Alaric and Miss McKnee smiled at each other once again. Finally, they could finish the dance they had begun so many years before.

When the music stopped, the people standing around the couple cheered and applauded. Even Miss McKnee's dog barked happily. I let go of the record player and slipped the *Dancing to the Vienna Waltz* record back into its sleeve. Then, exhausted, I passed out!

Strauss's bat

The next day, Shadow Mansion looked exactly like it had before Count Alaric and Ipanema had moved in. The windows were closed and the front door was boarded up.

There was no trace of its former tenants or Miss McKnee. Becca went to Miss McKnee's house to look for her, but the house was locked. When she went to her dance class that evening, there was a note hanging on the school's door that read:

ALL CLASSES ARE CANCELLED UNTIL
FURTHER NOTICE.

– Miss McKnee

Becca was devastated. She shoved her leotard into the back of a drawer and swore that she would never dance again. I felt terrible. But what could I do?

Fortunately, the situation became clear a few days later. An envelope addressed to Becca and a package addressed to me arrived at the Silvers' house. Both were postmarked from Brazil!

Becca opened the envelope and pulled out the letter. "It's a letter from Miss McKnee," she exclaimed. I leaned over her shoulder to read the letter.

Dear Becca,

Please forgive me for leaving like that, but Count Alaric didn't even give me time to pack my suitcases! He desperately needed a holiday somewhere warm and sunny (he's always so pale!), and had promised to take Ipanema back to Brazil.

Don't worry, dear, I'll be back in the spring, and I'll see you then. I'm not leaving the school and, most importantly, I'm not leaving a promising student like you!

See you soon,

Miss McKnee

Becca started bouncing around the room.

"Miss McKnee's coming back!" she squealed. "Miss McKnee's coming back!"

I opened my package too. It contained a postcard and a CD. The postcard showed a white sandy beach, palm trees, and a clear blue sea. On the other side, it read:

Dear Echo,

Count Alaric has finally kept his promise to take me back home to Brazil. Thank you! I couldn't have done it without your help. Will you come and see me sometime? I'm counting on it!

A hug goodbye!

Ipanema

P.S. I've attached the recipe for my new dish. It's called "Boom Boom Rice". Tell Tyler that it's even hotter than the other one!

P.P.S. The CD is from Count Alaric. It's by a

famous composer named Strauss. He's the same man who wrote The Blue Danube, *and this one is dedicated to a bat. That's Count Alaric's way of saying thank you.*

Things have gone back to normal around here now. Or at least as normal as things can be for the Bat Pack. Becca has been dancing from dusk to dawn every day. She even decided to teach Tyler how to waltz. I can always tell when they're practising – the entire house starts shaking!

Needless to say, I'm still Becca's best dance partner. I bet you're not surprised, are you?

As for me, I've been listening to Strauss's *The Bat* over and over. It's quite inspiring and really gets my creative juices flowing. In fact, I just finished writing the horror story I'd promised to Michael. It's about a vampire who falls in love with a dance teacher. He had danced an unforgettable waltz with her many years ago and is desperate to find her again. Do you think he'll like it?

A *dancing* goodbye, from yours truly,

ABOUT THE AUTHOR

Roberto Pavanello is an accomplished children's author and teacher. He currently teaches Italian at school and is an expert in children's theatre. Pavanello has written many children's books, including *Dracula and the School of Vampires*, *Look I'm Calling the Shadow Man!*, and the Bat Pat series, which has been published in Spain, Belgium, Holland, Turkey, Brazil, Argentina, China, the United States, and now the United Kingdom as Echo and the Bat Pack. He is also the author of the Oscar & Co. series, as well as the Flambus Green books. Pavanello currently lives in Italy with his wife and three children.

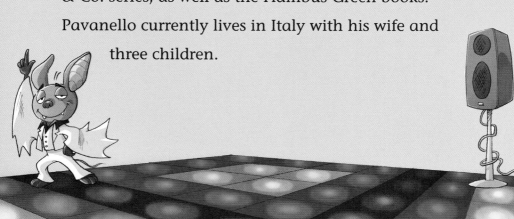

GLOSSARY

aerobatics skilful or dangerous movements performed in the sky

coincidence chance happening or meeting

disastrous causing distress or injury

magnificent very impressive or beautiful

obvious easy to see and understand

rickety old, weak, and likely to break

spectacular remarkable or dramatic

tenant someone who rents a room, a house, an apartment, an office, or land that belongs to someone else

DISCUSSION QUESTIONS

1. Miss McKnee teaches Becca lots of new dances, including the waltz. Talk about some other types of dances you know.

2. Ipanema is from Brazil, a country in South America. Have you ever been to a foreign country? Talk about one you would like to visit.

3. My friends all have different hobbies. Becca likes to dance, Michael likes to read, and Tyler likes to invent things. Talk about some of your favourite hobbies.

WRITING PROMPTS

1. Becca is determined to teach me and her brothers how to dance. Write about a time you tried to teach someone something new. What was it? How did you go about it?

2. Write about the Debutante Ball from the perspective of one of the guests. How would you react to seeing a real live vampire?

3. When our new neighbour moved in on Friday Street, I was a real scaredy-bat! Write about what you would have done to investigate.

Check out more
Mysteries and
Adventures with
Echo and the Bat Pack